Bon Voyage, Mister Rodriguez

Christiane Duchesne
& François Thisdale

pajamapress

First published in Canada and the United States in 2019

Text copyright © 2019 Christiane Duchesne
Illustration copyright © 2019 François Thisdale
This edition copyright © 2019 Pajama Press Inc.
This is a first edition.

10 9 8 7 6 5 4 3 2 1

 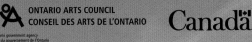

The publisher gratefully acknowledges the support of the Canada Council for the Arts and the
Ontario Arts Council for its publishing program. We acknowledge the financial support of the
Government of Canada through the Canada Book Fund (CBF) for our publishing activities.

Library and Archives Canada Cataloguing in Publication

Title: Bon voyage, Mister Rodriguez / Christiane Duchesne & [illustrated by] François Thisdale.
Names: Duchesne, Christiane, 1949- author. | Thisdale, François, 1964- illustrator.
Identifiers: Canadiana 20190086246 | ISBN 9781772780895 (hardcover)
Classification: LCC PS8557.U265 B66 2019 | DDC jC813/.54—dc23

Publisher Cataloging-in-Publication Data (U.S.)
Names: Duchesne, Christiane, 1949-, author. | Thisdale, François, 1964-, illustrator.
Title: Bon Voyage, Mister Rodriguez / Christiane Duchesne & François Thisdale.
Description: Toronto, Ontario Canada : Pajama Press, 2019. | Summary: "An imaginative explo-
ration of a community preparing for the death of an aged member. Every day, the children wait to
watch the fascinating Mr. Rodriguez go by. When he flies off on his piano, they know it's time to
say goodbye"— Provided by publisher.
Identifiers: ISBN 978-1-77278-089-5 (hardcover)
Subjects: LCSH: Death – Juvenile fiction. | Farewells – Juvenile fiction. | Children and death –
Juvenile fiction. | BISAC: JUVENILE FICTION / Mysteries & Detective Stories. | JUVENILE
FICTION / Social Themes / Death, Grief, Bereavement.
Classification: LCC PZ7.D834Bon |DDC [E] – dc23

Original art created with acrylic and digital media
Cover and book design—Rebecca Bender

Manufactured by Qualibre Inc./Printplus
Printed in China

Pajama Press Inc.
181 Carlaw Ave. Suite 251 Toronto, Ontario Canada, M4M 2S1

Distributed in Canada by UTP Distribution
5201 Dufferin Street Toronto, Ontario Canada, M3H 5T8

Distributed in the U.S. by Ingram Publisher Services
1 Ingram Blvd. La Vergne, TN 37086, USA

To F. T. and to Carolyn Perkes for her
excellent translation —C.D.

To my mom, 1933-2019 —F.T.

EVERY AFTERNOON AT FOUR O'CLOCK,
Mister Rodriguez stepped out of a narrow laneway
and strolled through the street. To us, it looked as if
he had clouds under his coat. Or maybe balloons.

Every day, we would hide
behind the trunk of an oak
tree and wait for the old
man to pass by.

One Monday, at exactly four o'clock, Mister Rodriguez stepped into the street—and stopped. He looked left and right. Then he looked down, as if to check the position of his feet.

We held our breath. Was he waiting for someone? Although we could not say why, we knew that today would be different.

A dove fluttered down and settled on the tip of his shoe. Very gently, Mister Rodriguez attached a fine silk thread around her foot…and off they went!

On Tuesday, Mister Rodriguez floated down the street with a fishbowl carefully balanced on his head.

On Wednesday, an old sheepdog slowly approached him. Mister Rodriguez settled the weary dog into a sled, and together they slipped down the street.

We wondered...what would happen on Thursday? None of the adults seemed to notice Mister Rodriguez coming and going.

On Thursday, a cat slowly limped up
to Mister Rodriguez. He tied a pair of
wings to the old kitty's back.

On Friday, a piano appeared on the
street. Mister Rodriguez sat down,
and a fine melody flowed out to sea.

On Saturday, Mister Rodriguez did not show up at all. This had never happened before. We searched and searched, but we could not find him.

Perhaps Mister Rodriguez had changed his routine? On Sunday, we arrived early in the morning to wait for him.

Suddenly he appeared out
of nowhere, far above us.
He was not alone.

He winked and pointed to the
clouds in the distance.

We never saw Mister Rodriguez after that. He had gone away, probably forever. But we knew he was happy.

So we left a message in the sand.